Pete the Cat
SECRET AGENT
TOP SECRET
by Kimberly & James Dean
HARPER
An Imprint of HarperCollinsPublishers

Pete the Cat: Secret Agent
 For information address HarperCollins Children's Books, a division of HarperCollins Publishers, 195 Broadway, New York, NY 10007.
www.harpercollinschildrens.com

Library of Congress Control Number: 2019950257
ISBN 978-0-06-286842-8

Typography by Jeanne Hogle
21 22 23 CWM 5 4 3 2
❖
First Edition

Look!

Can you spot Secret Agent Meow?

He's the coolest spy in town. No one knows that Agent Meow's true identity is Pete the Cat. Not even Bob!

Agent Meow is an expert at solving cases.
Last year, he caught the Ruby Robber.

"My favorite necklace!"

Two weeks ago, he found the missing key to town.

"You've saved the town again!"
CAT CITY
MAYOR

Escape Hatch
Experimental Rocket
Hidden Elevator
Exit Tunnel
Meow-Mobile
CAT
Laboratory and Spy Gadgets
Snack Room
Skateboard Practice Room

Agent Meow works in a top secret location. The only way to unlock the door is with his pawprint. Inside, he has a lot of very groovy gadgets.

AGENT MEOW'S UNDERGROUND HEADQUARTERS

The meow-mobile can take Agent Meow anywhere at lightning speed.

It can turn into a car, a helicopter,

and even a skateboard.

Agent Meow also has a supercool spy watch camera. It looks like an ordinary watch. But with one click, it's anything but ordinary.

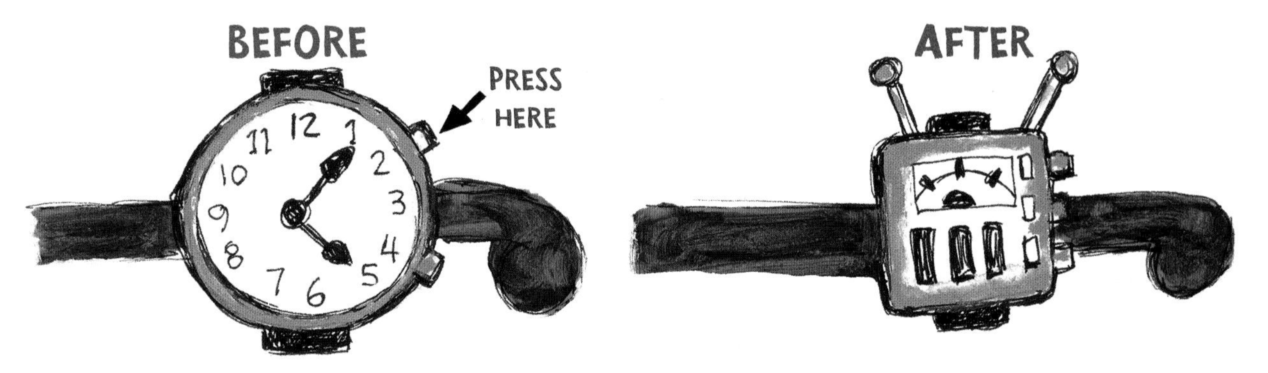
BEFORE
PRESS HERE
AFTER

He just created his own flying listening device so he can hear everything, even when he's not near. He calls it his secret-catcher.

Sometimes when Agent Meow is on a mission, he wears a disguise.

Once Agent Meow coated himself in paint to blend into a painting.

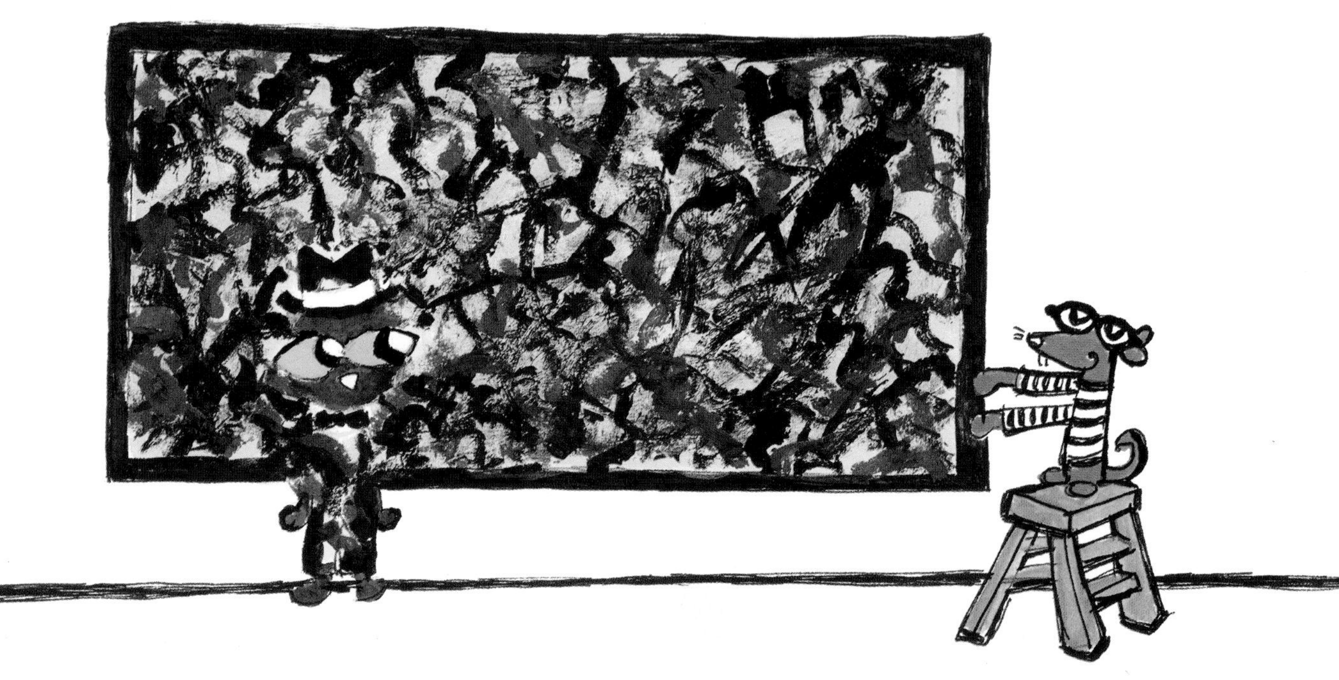

Another time, he pretended to be a tree.
A bird family built a nest on his head.
He's a cat undercover!

One morning, Agent Meow is flying his secret-catcher when he hears a surprising message.

Agent Meow can't tell who is talking because there is too much static, but he hears,

"Super-secret rendezvous . . . seven p.m. tonight . . . You know where to meet."

Agent Meow is very intrigued.

He needs to fine-tune his secret-catcher so he can hear better next time. He heads to the hardware store. He takes a shortcut through the park.

SHORT-CUT
The LONG WAY

Time is of the essence when you're a spy!

Agent Meow spots a group of people whispering by the swings.

Why would anyone come to the park and not play on the swings? he wonders.

He disguises himself so he can get closer.

CAT
TOP SECRET
CAT

HARPER
An Imprint of HarperCollinsPublishers
www.harpercollinschildrens.com

"Tonight is going to be huge," says Squirrel.

"I really hope we can pull it off," says Octopus. "What should I bring?"

"Go ask Grumpy Toad," says Squirrel. "He knows the plan."

Grumpy Toad works at the library! Agent Meow knows exactly where to go next.

CAT

The library is very quiet, so Agent Meow tiptoes around the bookshelves.

Good thing he knows a secret hiding spot inside the bookcase.

He pulls on his favorite book, and it leads to an underground hideaway.

Finally, he spots Grumpy Toad whispering to Gus.

He pulls out his secret-catcher.

"Do we need anything else for tonight?"
"No, that's all right. Turtle is already at the market. He's picking up stuff for me!"

Agent Meow knows he will never make it to the market before Turtle leaves.

At least not without his meow-mobile!

Whoosh!

"Aha! Suspect Turtle spotted," says Agent Meow. Good thing he remembered to bring his old-fashioned binoculars. "Looks like he is buying gallons of banana ice cream. . . . But why is Callie there too?"

Agent Meow turns on his secret-catcher. He hears Callie and Turtle talking.

"I found Grumpy Toad's fish sticks."
"Cool, now let's get going. We can't be late to Gus's house."
CAT CITY MARKET

Agent Meow checks his watch. He has to move fast!
He hops onto his meow-mobile and ZOOMS over.

Whoosh!

It's only ten minutes until it's seven p.m.!

What could the secret meeting be about? Agent Meow wonders. He'll need the perfect disguise—one that will blend in.

He tries several hats . . .

glasses . . .

and even a wig.

Suddenly he gets the perfect idea. He will go as Pete the Cat! No one will expect him.

Agent Meow tries to whistle and act cool as he walks by Gus's house.

Yet he can't help but feel a little nervous. He walks up to the house. It seems quiet. Too quiet.

"Surprise!" everyone yells.

"It's a surprise birthday party for you!" says Callie. "We got all your favorite food, like fish sticks and banana ice cream."

HAPPY BIRTHDAY
FISH STICKS

"How did you know it was my birthday?" asks Agent Meow.
"You can't keep a secret from us," says Gus.

!!!
BANANA
ICE
CREAM

Pete the Cat may be able to keep his secret identity, Agent Meow, hidden from his friends, but he definitely can't keep his birthday a secret.

"This is best surprise party of all time!"

HAPPY BIRTHDAY